Emma Huntington Nason

The Tower

With Legends and Lyrics

Emma Huntington Nason

The Tower
With Legends and Lyrics

ISBN/EAN: 9783744787406

Printed in Europe, USA, Canada, Australia, Japan

Cover: Foto ©Andreas Hilbeck / pixelio.de

More available books at **www.hansebooks.com**

THE TOWER

WITH LEGENDS AND LYRICS

BY

EMMA HUNTINGTON NASON

BOSTON AND NEW YORK
HOUGHTON, MIFFLIN AND COMPANY
The Riverside Press, Cambridge
1895

The Riverside Press, Cambridge, Mass., U. S. A.
Electrotyped and Printed by H. O. Houghton & Co.

DEDICATED TO C. H. N.

THE TOWER

I AM the tower of Belus — the tower of old
      am I !
Under the rifting lines of the gloaming's trem-
      ulant sky,
Under the shifting signs of the ages circling by,
I stand in the might of the mighty — the tower
      of Belus, I !
Who are these at my feet like pygmies scorched
      in the sun ?
Who, but the petty hordes of a race that has
      just begun ?
It matters little to me whether prince or Bed-
      ouin stand,
Or the lizard creep at my feet, or the jackal
      up from the sand !
What does the time-bound traveler know of the
      dim by-gone ?
What can he tell of the glory that died with
      the world's bright dawn,
More than the son of the desert ? the slim,
      green creeping things ?

The night-owl, fast in his crevice? the bat, with
    his ghostly wings?
Each in his own way imagines the past and the
    yet-to-be;
Each to himself is greatest; equal alike to me!
I am the tower of Belus; ages unnumbered are
    mine;
Mightier I than the gods who dreamed them-
    selves divine!

Is this the grandest of rivers that rolled like a
    king to the sea,
Crying, "I am the great Euphrates! bring all
    your tithes unto me"?
How the ships with their treasured freight went
    down to their rocky bed!
Are there ghouls, insatiate still, with grinning
    mouths to be fed,
That you burst your stony embankments, rav-
    aging meadow and fen,
Making drearier drear desolation, in scorn for
    the arts of men?
Ah! Babylonia, where — ah! where is thy fruit-
    ful plain,
Spreading sea-like unto the ocean its billowy
    fields of grain?

Where now is the mighty city, secure .with its
    brazen gates,
And walls on whose towering fastness the Assy-
    rian warrior waits,
His milk-white steeds in war-gear, his blazoned
    flags unfurled,
Hurling with grim defiance his challenge out
    to the world ?
Where are the toiling millions who wrought,
    with their cunning skill,
Sweet dreams of a fair ideal, in forms that were
    fairer still ?
Oh, Babylon's looms are silent; in silence
    dead are the plains ;
And dead are city and soldier; the tower
    alone remains.

I am the tower of Belus ! I stand in the grasp
    of fate !
I,. and proud Babylon's princess ; together we
    watch and wait,
She for her lover's returning ; I for oblivion's
    knell ;
And which with the greater longing, the heav-
    ens alone can tell.
Is there any joy in existence void of hope or
    of fears,

In painless, slow dissolution through thousands
    of weary years?
Or rest for the ghost of the maiden that alike
    in life and in death,
While years into centuries ripen, and centuries
    wane, keeps faith?
She counts not night nor morning, but each
    new moon to greet,
She cometh with shadowy garments whose per-
    fume, subtle and sweet,
From balms forever forgotten, floats over her
    lover's low bed,
Where he, impatient, is sleeping the sleep of
    the restless dead.
For had he not said, "Beloved, come at the
    mystical hour,
When the young moon lightens with silver the
    shade of the mighty tower"?
Had he not sworn, "Though I perish! though
    Belus lie in the dust!"—
And the trust of a loving woman is blind and
    unending trust.

Three hands were joined at their parting, three
    voices breathing love's breath;

The voice of the third was ghostly, its hand
    was the hand of death :
And the white stone goddess had shivered while
    the glow of the sunset dyes
Deepened in one broad blood - streak and
    blazed in the western skies ;
But the maid, unheeding the omen, hears only
    her lover's last oath,
Nor dreams that his life has been purchased
    with this, as he dieth for both.
The grave that is reeking with vengeance no tale
    of its mystery brings :
Gods ! — he was a Tyrian soldier ! she, the
    daughter of kings !
And what but death can be reckoned as price
    of unequal love ?
And what but the vow, recorded by direful
    fates above,
Could save the life of the maiden ? — the vow
    that never again,
While the tower of mighty Belus o'ershadows
    the haunts of men,
With its ancient and storied grandeur — ay,
    more ! that never the while
One upright stone shall be standing alight with
    the young moon's smile,

Shall body or ghost of the soldier under its
    shadow wait : —
But death is longer than life-time ; and love is
    stronger than fate !

There were hope e'en yet for the tower, stand-
    ing stark and alone,
Had the flames of an altar-fire e'er burned in
    its heart of stone ;
Had the depths of its adamant bosom e'er
    thrilled with a love or hate,
Stern destiny's grip must have slackened, slack-
    ened sooner or late.
I am the tower of Belus ! Can the story be
    written, " I was " ?
Shall the tide of an ended existence flow back
    to the primal cause
Which sent it first into being ? and records of
    age sublime
In utter nothingness vanish under the finger of
    time ?
Hist ! a jar in the ragged brickwork ! it totters,
    and now is still ;
I can feel the sand slow trickling, with a cold
    unearthy thrill ;
Perchance but a stone is falling — perchance
    it is death's last throe —

Ay ! under the young moon's glitter I catch the
    roseate glow
Of the maiden's royal mantle ; and the clang of
    a mailèd tread
Tells that the past has canceled its debt which
    held the dead.
He cometh with step triumphant ! he readeth
    the fateful sign :
The last grim arch is shattered which linked
    their lot with mine.

Ah, fate, to the last relentless ! thy vassal
    allegiance owns —
Go back to your cities, O stranger ! write,
    " Belus a heap of stones ! "

BODY AND SOUL.

HERE at life's silent, shadowy gate,
O Soul, my Soul, I lie and wait ;
Faint in the darkness, blind and dumb,
O Soul, my promised comrade, come !

The morn breaks gladly in the east ;
Hush ! hark ! the signs of solemn feast ;
The softened footstep on the stair ;
The happy smile, the chant, the prayer ;
The dainty robes, the christening bowl —
'T is well with Body and with Soul.

Why lingerest thou at dawn of life ?
Seest not a world with pleasure rife ?
Hear'st not the song and whir of bird ?
The joyous leaves to music stirred ?
Thou too shalt sing and float in light ;
My Soul, thou shalt be happy — quite.

But yet so young and such unrest ?
Thou must be glad, my glorious guest !

Here is the revel, here is mirth;
Here strains enchanting sway the earth; —
Measures of joy in fullness spent;
My Soul, thou canst but be content.

Is this a tear upon my hand?
A tear? I do not understand.
Ripples of laughter, and a moan?
Why sit we thus apart, alone?
Lift up thine eyes, O Soul, and sing!
He comes, our lover, and our king!
Feel how each pulse in rapture thrills!
Look, at our feet the red wine spills!
And he — he comes with step divine,
A spirit meet, O Soul, for thine.

Body and Soul's supremest bliss —
What, dost thou ask for more than this?

Stay, here are houses, lands, and gold;
Here, honor's hand; here, gains untold;
Drink thou the full cup to the lees;
Drink, Soul, and make thy bed in ease.
Thou art my prisoner; thou, my slave;
And thou *shalt* sip wherein I lave.

Nay? nay?   Then there are broader fields,
Whose luring path a treasure yields ;
Thou shalt the universe explore,
Its heights of knowledge, depths of lore ;
Shalt journey far o'er land and sea ;
And I, my Soul, will follow thee ;
Will follow — follow — but I lag ;
My heart grows faint, my footsteps flag.

And there are higher, holier things ?
Is this a taunt thy spirit flings ?
What is it, Soul, that thou wouldst say ?
Thou erst had time to fast and pray.
Give me one word, one loving sign,
For this spent life of yours and mine !

I held thee fast by sordid ties ?
I trailed thy garments, veiled thine eyes ?
Go on, I come : but once did wait,
O Soul, for thee, at morning's gate.
Canst thou not pause to give me breath ?
Perchance this shadow, Soul, is death.
I stumble, fall ; it is the grave ;
I am the prisoner ; I the slave ;
And thou, strange guest, for aye art free ;
Forgive me, Soul !   I could but be

The earth that soiled, the fleshly clod,
The weight that bound thee to the sod.

Dust unto dust! I hear the knell;
And yet, O Soul, I loved thee well!

TWO FACES.

WHEN that enchanted tapestry unrolls
   The pictures wrought in old Homeric song,
Where heroes wrestle with their dual souls
   Who, born of gods, do yet to earth belong ;

Where white-armed women ply the wondrous
     looms,
   While long-haired Greek or crested Trojan
     falls ;
Where desolation sits in lofty rooms,
   And old men weep upon the fated walls ;

Where skies are red with glare of burning
     pile,
   Of cities sacked, of beakëd ships aflame ;
Where gods insatiate bend with awful smile,
   Above the countless hecatombs of slain ;

Where that superb procession of the past
   Sweeps through the ages, and with noiseless
     tread

Marches and countermarches, till at last
   I seem myself to stand among the dead ;

Then two young faces, vivid and intense,
   Enthrall my spirit wheresoe'er I turn ;
Two visions sweet of girlish innocence,
   Of eyes that shine, of cheeks that pale and
      burn.

And them I follow through the fitful light
   That weirdly shifts o'er human grief and
      joy,
E'en as they follow, from her chamber white,
   The Argive Helen to the walls of Troy.

Silent they watch, with widely wondering eyes,
   Her tender tears at Menelaus' name,
Discerning there that olden sad surprise,
   Immortal beauty and immortal shame.

Silent they wait, these maids-in-waiting sweet :
   What sudden thoughts within your bosoms
      stir,
O mute companions, as at Helen's feet,
   Ye watch the life-tide ebb and flow for
      her ?

What part have ye in jealousy and hate,
    In love and loss and sin's unseemly woe?
Alas! Of all the mysteries of fate,
    There is not one ye shall not live to know!

Across life's web the shuttle rainbow-hued
    No more henceforth can send its stainless
        thread;
A dull red seam, with this day's blight imbued,
    Marks woman's faith despoiled and lying
        dead.

And no dread picture on the ancient page
    So moves my being, — ah! not even he,
The great Achilles, awful in his rage,
    Nursing his wrath beside the wailing sea;

Nor fair Andromache, who through her tears
    Holds up her boy again and yet again
For that farewell which, ringing through the
        years,
    Makes women weep and men once more be
        men;

Nor, where the fount of swift Scamander runs,
    The glorious Hector falters for relief;

Not aged Priam, spoiled of many sons ; .
   Not Hecuba, still royal in her grief ;

But, uneclipsed by all the mighty shades,
   Your faces haunt me, threatened by the
      Fates,   .
Æthra and Clymene, — O silent maids,
   Who stand with Helen at the Scæan gates !

SHOES OF ALABASTER.

From Agra, city of delight,
   These tiny shoes have come to me,
Of alabaster carven white,
   With clasp and chasery.

They found them at the temple door
   Where opal clouds swing low and swirl,
Like kindred shapes, to hover o'er
   Thy domes, O Mosque of Pearl!

Who left them at that glorious gate?
   For plaint or prayer of what fair maid
Were these frail wonders doomed to wait
   Outside the sacred shade?

I see her linger in the glow,
   Where sunlit tulips sway and meet;
The milk-white marbles warmer grow
   To lure her dainty feet.

I see her pass within the shrine
   Whose walls are like to Paradise ;
Their jeweled scrolls, with text divine,
   Are envious of her eyes.

Her gentle footfall leaves no sound
   Within the calm and holy fane ;
Her lovers, prostrate on the ground,
   Shall wait for her in vain.

For never mortal maid was she,
   But some white wraith of fancy's muse,
Some dream-child born of ecstasy,
   Who wore these flawless shoes.

With pointed tips set toward the East,
   Here in the sunlight they shall rest,
Until, from her long fast, or feast,
   Shall come their spirit-guest.

White ghosts of shoes ! speed if ye must
   When she shall call ; but leave, I pray,
Two flakes of alabaster dust,
   To show she passed this way.

THE FIRST GREEK PORTRAIT.

So very long ago it was, men have forgot the
    year,
And yet the time of myrtle-bloom to lovers
    then was dear;
The waves were then as blue as now that
    washed the Sicyon shore,
The olive's shade, as gray and green, above
    the open door,
Where stood the ancient potter's wheel, with
    vase and urn of clay,
Simply, and yet so chastely wrought, men have
    forgot the way.
The daffodils and hyacinths beneath the gray
    wall grew,
O'er which the wild Corinthian grape its tan-
    gled blossom threw;
And there the handsome, glad young Greek
    the potter's daughter wooed,
In days when maids were dear as now, and
    men as brave and good.
He said, "Farewell — ah, sweet — farewell!"
    and yet he did not go;

Old is the fashion, very old, but still its ways
    we know;
And longingly and lovingly his shadow on the
    wall
Swayed in the sunlight, went and came, as
    shadows flit and fall,
Till suddenly — a profile clear upon the dark-
    ened space —
The young Greek girl, with hand inspired,
    had drawn her lover's face.

The potter marveled when he found the shadow
    pictured there:
"'T is from the gods, a gift," he said, "to
    shape our soul's despair!"
And reverently he filled the lines, which limned
    the portrait old,
With yellow clay from Corinth's strand and
    sacred kept the mould;
While all the Sicyon potters came to learn, by
    look or sign,
How haply to Butades' child befell this touch
    divine.
And through the world the wonder went; but
    idle now her fame : —
It was so very long ago, men have forgot her
    name!

Ah! great Apelles! what didst thou — thou
    son of Sicyon's heart!
Proud heir of all to Greece bequeathed by this
    one maiden's art —
That thou hast not remembered her, when
    glorious in the land?
What face so dear as hers had been from thy
    immortal hand?
And Myron grand! and Phidias! had ye no
    debt to own?
No memory to cast in bronze, no grace to
    carve in stone,
To mind us of this fair Greek maid, of all her
    race the first
To teach: Love is the fount of art for which
    the nations thirst?
Your gods are many! Great they stand! We
    bow before their shrine;
And yet we would there might have been, in
    all the glorious line,
One simply carven monument, whereon we still
    might trace:
To her who erst on Sicyon's wall outlined her
    lover's face!

A GHOST.

This is Pavia! Grand old town
Of priestly lore and state renown.
This is Pavia! let us stay
Our weary feet one night and day.
The city of an hundred towers,
Its great heart still will shelter ours;
Its walls are shadowy, cool, and gray;
Here let us rest one night and day.

Beneath these arches, grim and quaint,
Still lies the dust of Sage and Saint,
Whose ashes for a thousand years
Have shrined the pilgrim's fitful tears.
Men idly come and idly go —
What is it that affrights me so?
Some awful presence in the air,
Ghost-like and chill, seems everywhere.
Pavia? Naught is in the word!
What have I read? what have I heard?
Who beckons when I fain would wait
At Belcredi, or Maino's gate?

Who follows when my footsteps stray
Within thy courts, San Michelé?
Who glides before through hall and fane
Founded of old by Charlemagne?
By Charlemagne?   Ah, now I know,
Stand back I pray, and let me go!
Where his great deeds in splendor shine,
Still lurk the sin and shame of thine.
Thy dread name, I recall at last,
Thou saddest ghost of all the past!

Ay! thou wert Queen! the last to hold
That title proud in Wessex old!
Thou wert Eadburgha — yes, I see
The empty cup thou handest me.
Too late, alas, my scanty dole
To ease the hunger of a soul!
Thou gav'st thy husband's friend to sup,
And mixed for him the poisoned cup.
The brave king quaffed at foaming brim;
Young Warr, his liege, drank after him,
And both fell dead!   Oh, tale of woe!
Begun long centuries ago!

And o'er the seas to Charlemagne
Thou fled'st for comfort, but in vain.

He gently bade the sweet nuns call
Thee, Lady of the Convent Hall;
But thy seared soul found naught of good
Amidst the saintly sisterhood;
So driven on, and up and down,
From cloister-gate to tower and town,
Thou cam'st, at last, with bleeding feet,
To tread Pavia's ancient street;
Here doomed to beg forevermore
Thy bitter bread from door to door.

Here thou didst die with hunger's wail;
I would I could forget the tale!
I would to-night I did not know
Thy wan shape flitting to and fro;
Thy cup once drained, no hand could fill;
That cup accurst is empty still!
Too late, alas, my scanty dole
To ease the hunger of a soul!
May God's grace rest thee at the last,
Thou saddest ghost of all the past!

Pavia! Ah, I would not stay
Within thy walls one night or day!

THE MOUNTAIN OF THE HOLY CROSS.

THE Lord himself hath set the sign!—
"Dear Christ forgive!" God's servant prayed;
And every head along the line
Of bronzed, rough-bearded men was bare,
In sudden silence, as the prayer
Arose within the mission-glade.

Before, behind, the mountains stood;
In grim, defiant strength arrayed,
They seemed an awful brotherhood,
Through some gigantic passion knit;
Too great for earth; for heaven unfit;
"Dear Christ forgive!" God's servant prayed.

And lo! beyond the wild ravine,
Where ghostly pines their gray arms toss,
A hoary mountain head was seen,
Whose fissured crest forever shows,
Emblazoned in eternal snows,
The sacred emblem of the Cross.

24

And men who called the world accurst,
And men who ne'er had heard a prayer,
Men who had dared and done their worst,
Rode awestruck through the lonely way,
Forgetting what they fain would say,
With Christ's own sign before them there.

Then slowly up the mountain track,
Wind-swept, the rude procession swayed ;
Nor, though long summers waned, came back.
Died they beneath the holy sign
Of earth-love crowned by the divine ?
" We hope through Christ ! " God's servant
       prayed.

The Lord himself the Cross hath set !
Was the Omniscient One afraid
Lest his far-straying sons forget ?
Lest they, who midst the mountains hide,
Remember not the Crucified ?
" Dear Christ, forbid ! " God's servant prayed.

SLUMBER SONG.

Calm, unimpassioned, in thy wide dominions,
   Wilt thou relentless stay, and staying keep
The restful shadows of thy purple pinions
   Aloof from mortals, O sweet goddess, Sleep?

We know the twilight brought thy soft caresses,
   But toil forbade us, and we might not rest;
We saw white poppies braided in thy tresses,
   We breathed their fragrance, leaning on thy
      breast;

Yet dared not stay lest, drowsy at its coming,
   We mock the midnight — and the watch was
      set;
We longed to clasp thee, but some chill, be-
      numbing
Presence withheld us, and withholds us yet.

Art thou so grieved that like some slighted
      maiden,
   Thou'lt not return though we repentant weep,

And pray for balms, in Lotos islands laden
　　With　slumberous　airs, O　gentle　goddess,
　　　Sleep ?

Or, vigil-worn, do thy obscure relations
　　To man's dull senses faintly die away ?
And have we left no mystic incantations
　　To lure thee back, no charm to bid thee stay ?

Ah ! I recall one old song's drowsy measure,
　　A rhythmic murmur to a baby fair ;—
Once　more,　sweet　goddess,　bend　at　mortal
　　　pleasure !
　　Shake out the blossoms　from thy lustrous
　　　hair !

"We float, we float !" a mother sang and sing-
　　　ing,
　　Rocked to and fro and swayed her baby love ;
"White spray swings upward to the blue waves
　　　clinging ;
　　White clouds drift downward from the blue
　　　above.

"The great waves rise with steady undulations ;
　　The　great　waves　fall ; we　lie　upon　their
　　　, breast ;

We hold our hearts to check their wild pulsa-
      tions,
   We clasp our hands — but rest, my baby,
      rest!

"Thou hast no care!   Thou need'st not wake
      or worry
   Should moons go eastward or should moons
      go west;
What couldst thou do though stars should wait
      or hurry,
   In their long courses?   Rest, my baby, rest!

"It is not time, until some far to-morrow,
   For thee to strive with Why and Whence and
      How;
Leave the great world to hug its load of sor-
      row
   In bitterness! Sleep, baby love, sleep now!

"We float, we float!" she sang; and, with her,
      singing,
   My soul keeps tune, repeating still the cry,
"What couldst thou do though stars astray
      were swinging?"
   Ah, little one! and what indeed could I?

I lay me down and leave till God's to-morrow
  Earth's vexing problems with their stern be-
      quest,
Since rest is duty! and I fain would borrow
  The mother-music for my spirit's guest.

And lo! she comes! As in the old time
      plighted,
  Once more we float, through Dreamland
      shadows deep;
We did not know, until our souls were righted,
  How vain our watching, nor how blest our
      sleep.

WINDS OF THE NORTH.

THE cold winds out of the Northland blow,
Filling the frosty air with snow,
Sweeping the white flakes to and fro,
    O'er the moorlands dreary;
My lord, he wills that the flames burn higher,
My lady, around the glowing fire,
Draweth her crimson cushions nigher,
    Calling it cheery.

I am out in the gardens old,
Out in the bitter, stinging cold,
Smiling to see the gathering mould
    On the brown leaves lying;
Drinking with joy the breath of the breeze
That sweeps through the boughs of the leafless
    trees,
The breath of the wind from the Northern Seas
    To the dead flowers sighing.

Let them bar their door to the Northwind bold,
Round them closer their garments fold,

Shudder as when a tale is told
     Of the dead and dying;
The doors of my heart I open throw,
Through its empty portals come and go,
O wild Northwinds, for I love ye so,
     With a love defying!

Were ye not born in that land of mine,
Rocked in the arms of the Northern pine,
Kissed by the leaves of the Upland vine
     Which icily glisten?
Have I not come in the gloom to-night,
Out in the gloom which yet is bright,
With the fitful gleams of the Northern light,
     To lovingly listen?

Blow, glorious winds! for ye bring to me
A chant of the Northland strong and free,
With sweep of the skies, and surge of the sea,
     Through its measure flowing;
And clear in its rhythmical undertone,
I catch the airs to my childhood known,
The glad, wild songs that were mine alone,
     With the Northwinds blowing.

A MIRACLE

O RADIANT Life, when we set sail together,
    From out the mist-land, with your hand in
        mine
You vowed me all things ; days of sunlit weather,
    And nights of calm and skies of golden shine.

You said that I should drift by happy reaches
    Of shores low lying where the sea-bird flies ;
That I should watch, beyond white-sanded
        beaches,
    The glorious stars above the mountains rise.

That some day I should see the mystic token
    Which marked the harbor where my Love
        had been ;
Should see, and know my little boat was spoken,
    And with glad sails go flying swiftly in.

You promised, Life, that I should find the treas-
        ure
    Of which immortals long have dreamed and
        sung ;

The gift supreme — love's bliss in boundless
    measure !
  And I believed, for life and love were
    young.

Sit closer now, and clasp my hand more tightly !
  Nor hope, nor promise fails though years
    have fled,
But ah ! I see I took your vows too lightly,
  Too idly, Life ! I knew not what you said.

Safely you guided to the blessed haven
  My fragile craft; yet many a one went down
Whose hopes as eager were, nor wrong nor
    craven ;
  But swift storms whitened, and the rocks
    stood brown.

I know the ways where other voyagers drift-
    ing
  Beheld with joy the hilltops all a-gem ; —
Wrecked in the shadow of the heights uplift-
    ing,
  Tell me, O Life, what was 't thou promised
    them ?

Love's all! as unto me in that bright dawn-
    ing! —
  I tremble now to hold such rapture true!
It is a miracle! Yet I, at morning,
  Saw not the marvel, nor the wonder knew.

HADST THOU BUT TURNED.

SIR LANCELOT, turn back, turn back,
 I pray thee, from the lonely downs !
Why leavest thou the beaten track
 That leads to city, tower and towns ?
This way are footpaths rough and bare,
 With edge of moss or scanty fern ;
Beyond are meadows lush and fair : —
 Sir Lancelot, I pray thee turn !

Thou ridest with thy moody brain ;
 Thou ridest with thy sullen heart ;
Broad roads there are whose ways are plain ;
 Why seek the field that lies apart ?
Footpaths oft mean hearth-fires I trow,
 And meat and drink — and after that ?
Oh, after that — couldst thou but know,
 Thou wouldst not ride to Astolat.

Nor mist, nor hill can longer hide
 The castle-walls and turrets gray ;

Fair Astolat, thy gates were wide,
 Thy welcome boundless that fair day ;
And she, the " lily-maid," the child,
 Served graciously the guest — alack !
She had not raised her eyes and smiled,
 O Lancelot, hadst thou turned back !

She had not asked, she had not heard
 The witching tale of spur and plume :
She had not dared the sudden word
 That set the girlish cheeks abloom,
When, craving sweet consent of thine,
 She bounded up the castle stair,
And brought the red embroidered sign,
 O Lancelot, for thee to wear !

She had not watched thee ride away,
 Nor guarded, in that eastern tower,
Thy massive shield by night and day,
 Tracing each blazoned leaf and flower,
With throbbing heart and close-barred door,
 While she entranced and joyous sat,
Thy simplest word repeating o'er,
 Hadst thou not come to Astolat.

There had not dawned that bitter morn
 When woke the heart of sweet Elaine ;

And when, to crush the love new-born,
    Again the knight rode down the plain,
No scarlet sleeve flares on his helm,
    No farewell words he fondly saith;
The bravest peer of Arthur's realm
    Nor heeds, nor hears, the wail of death.

Ah, Lancelot! hadst thou not come
    To Astolat that woeful day,
The stainless dead, "steered by the dumb,"
    Had not in silence sailed away.
We had not watched the black-draped barge
    Float slowly toward the palace gate;
Nor seen, in stately halls and large,
    The lily-maiden audience wait.

We had not heard the rueful plea,
    (This, Lancelot, thou too shalt hear!)
" O peerless knight, pray thou for me!
    Pray thou for me, Queen Guinevere,
And give me burial, for the sake
    Of maiden love, unsought, unwed; —
Fear not, sweet Queen, I shall not wake!
    Farewell, Sir Knight, for I am dead!"

Nor had we wept, when all the train
    Moved up the aisle with solemn march,

To lay the golden-haired Elaine
   Beneath the grand cathedral arch ;
And yet, throughout the ages long,
   Our human hearts in vain had yearned
For England's saddest, sweetest song,
   O Lancelot, hadst thou but turned !

THE CASTLE OF SONG.

Upon the mountain height it stands,
In far-off, yet familiar lands.

Its outer walls are gray and cold,
Its sculptured gates are green with mould.

No warden from the watch-tower calls;
No bugle note of welcome falls.

Through garden paths, dark ivies twine,
With furze and heath and eglantine.

The hawthorn's branches bare and dry
Are sharply etched against the sky.

The dreary poplar casts a spell,
A dead and ghostly sentinel.

Within the empty banquet hall
Elusive footsteps flit and fall.

39

Who comes may wander at his will,
But finds each chamber cold and still,

Each corridor unswept and lone, —
Until the master claims his own.

Then he who holds the castle's key,
Wakes light and love and ecstasy!

In every hall the hearth-fires glow;
Fair youths and brave pass to and fro;

While stately ladies sit within,
Amidst their waiting-maids, and spin.

The happy bells, beneath the tower,
From dawn to dawn repeat the hour.

The May-time sends its messenger,   .
And violet banks are all astir.

The ivy for the rose makes room;
The hawthorn's boughs are white with bloom;

And lo!   Still wet with morning dew,
The Wonder-Flower of heavenly blue!

The glorious hours of day are spent
In knightly deed or tournament.

The lofty Bayards all are here,
Without reproach, without a fear.

At nightfall, to the chapel close,
The courtly train in reverence goes,

And fair nuns glide like shadows tall,
With pale moon-faces, through the hall; —

Cecilia, wrapt in holy calm;
Fair Hildegarde, with crown and palm;

And she the world remembereth,
The sweet girl saint, Elizabeth.

But when the vesper prayers are said,
The feast of song hath place instead.

With knight and prince on either hand,
The minstrel and the harper stand, —

The heroes of the Minnelay,
Reinmar the Old, Wolfram the Gray,

And he whom best we love to name,
Walther of fair Birdmeadow fame.

Who holds the castle's mystic key,
Lord of romance and song is he !

His vassals, every wave and breeze,
With treasure from beyond the seas !

And from his own watch tower afar,
His soul goes forth from star to star.

The heavens hang low — a scroll unsealed ;
The upper glories stand revealed.

Who holds the castle's mystic key,
The least of servitors is he !

He flings the portals open wide,
That all may enter and abide.

His bosom thrills with holy cheer ;
Will not the world be glad to hear ?

The great, wise world ?   It has no time
For wonder-tale or idle rhyme !

The great wise world?   It has no need
Heart-song, or star-song, e'er to heed !

Or if it chance a strain to hear,
It lists with unreceptive ear,

As if the castle did but seem, —
A fantasie, or foolish dream !

So floats the legend lightly on ;
A moment's gleam, and then 't is gone,

Like thistle-down upon the gale ! —
But simple folk believe the tale

Of wondrous, song-enchanted heights ;
And some have seen the castle-lights.

AT VESPERS.

THE vesper bells !
And sweet-faced nuns at even
Go in and out ; while clear the music swells,
Earth-born but tuned for heaven,
O vesper bells !

With folded hands,
The convent maidens meetly
Follow the train ; blessing the sacred bands
Which bind them, firmly, sweetly,
With folded hands.

And over them
Our Lady's eye beholding ;
Not e'en the winds dare kiss her mantle's hem,
Or flutter in its folding :
O sacred hem !

Up the dim aisles,
Beyond the studded portals,
Kneeling before the shrine where Mary smiles,

They pass, O happy mortals !
    Up the dim aisles.

    The golden sun,
Through painted windows stealing,
Throws shadows on the cheek of one ; for
    one
The bloom of rose revealing.
    O wayward sun !

    God only sees
How silent hearts are broken ;
The deepening flush, the Prince, on bended
    knees,
May trace — love's mystic token —
    On bended knees.

    Let grandest march
From organ old and solemn
Ring through the gloom of each receding arch,
    Around each fluted column !
    The Wedding March !

    Earth has a bride
To-day. Through misty veiling
Gleam love-lit eyes ; jewels and flowers hide

Within her silken trailing,
    Fair earth-born bride !

    But no less fair
Is she who on the morrow,
Kneels upon holy ground, in meekness there
    Asking surcease of sorrow ;
      Ah, no less fair !

    And this is all !
On strength divine relying,
The veiled head bows ; and sable curtains fall
    O'er human self-denying ;
      And this is all !

    With mortal eyes,
   We see.   Leave it for Him
To judge — in whom omniscient power lies —
    Whether the blight of earth shall dim
      The sacrifice.

UNTER DEN LINDEN.

JUNE 16, 1871.

I.

"VICTORY!" This was the first that she read :
And then, "Heart's dearest," the soldier had
      said,
Tracing the lines in a faltering way,
" Heart's dearest, the hospital surgeons say
That I shall be out of their hands to-day.
'T was an ugly wound, but the danger is past ;
I am coming to you, at last — at last !
Unter den Linden ! Yes, we shall be there !
Come with a rose in your dark shining hair —
Not the white blossoms you once used to wear.
White roses are meet for those who are slain ;
The rich wine-red, for the welcome, remain ;
Red as our life-blood, and sweet as the air
That floated from Eden, sweet and as rare ;
Greet me with a wine-red rose in your hair !
Germania triumphs ! Come with a song ;
And can you, dear heart, be patient and
      strong ?

For slow is the crutch and ghastly the sling,
And gone is the hand that once wore the
     ring —
Your ring, the one pledge I promised to bring!
I yield them ungrudged, with life, should need
     be,
But hold fast my troth to country and thee."

II.

In through the Brandenburg gateway they
     come,
With clashing of arms and clangor of drum!
Unter den Linden ! How proudly thy shade
Quivers and thrills with the wild cannonade,
As wild as the battle's carnival made!
Borne on its passion we catch up the song;
Thrilling and swelling, it thunders along;
Hear it, ye nations afar o'er the sea!
"Germania triumphs! Germania free —
Free and united through glad victory!"
Heroes of Saarbrück and Metz and Sedan
Tell how the torrent of victory ran!
Fair hands of women shall bring from afar
Hundreds of flowers for each bloody scar —
Scars that far dearer than rare jewels are.

"The Emperor comes!" for his guardsmen
    make way! —
"A woman, struck faint, has fallen," ye say?
And the troops, in their jubilant grand review,
March on through the linden-grown avenue ;
But she in her death-swoon still lieth there,
A woman stone white, yet passingly fair,
With the bloom of a wine-red rose in her hair.
Ah! what did ye hear the guardsman had
    said?
"Only a man, in the hospital, dead!"

LAVINIA.

A Painting by Titian in the Royal Museum at Berlin.

I COME once more to gaze on thee,
       Lavinia!
O'er miles and miles of weary sea,
Thy tender eyes have followed me;
I come once more to gaze on thee.
The long days crowd into the years,
And years die out with length of days,
While mocked alike are hopes and fears,
In life's perplexing, tangled ways,
Where men rush madly for the prize,
Which, lost or won, ne'er satisfies;
Yet never once, though stars may shine
Or shadows drift through skies of mine,
Can I forget the matchless grace
That lighteth up thy form and face;
The charm that baffles time and tide,
And holds me captive at thy side.

I am not skilled in artist-lore,   .

                Lavinia !

Of critic's phrase I bring no store,
The words fall soulless o'er and o'er ;
I am not skilled in artist-lore.
I only know the master's hand
Brings not such life from fancies dim ;
I know you stood as now you stand,
And gave the picture unto him.
I know the glory painted there
Hath glimmered in thy golden hair ;
I know the warm and tender brown
Hath nestled in thine amber gown.
I stand enraptured at thy feet ;
Hast thou no word of greeting sweet?
Thy lips have called though they be dumb ;
Lavinia, have I not come ?

I come to gaze into thine eyes,

                Lavinia !

I capture there the sweet surprise
That in their dusky shadow lies ;
I gaze and gaze into thine eyes.
'T were false to call thy face divine,
Life's perfectness is pictured there ;
The saints with heavenly beauty shine,

Thou of the earth art earthly fair.
Madonna like, a distant star
Might beckon me to realms afar ;
But thou, thou wouldst have walked with me,
Have led my steps right loyally
Through fragrant field or sterile dearth,
Hadst thou not come so soon to earth ;
Had I, untrammeled with my fate,
Not called to thee, alas, so late !

Wilt thou not wait in heaven for me,
                            Lavinia ?
A thousand years may only be
A single day, sweet friend, to thee ;
Wilt thou not wait in heaven for me ?
Long leagues of ocean seem to lie
Between me and the harbor-bar ;
Perchance thou canst not hear my cry
Across the billows, faint and far ;
Yet sometimes when the sea-foam falls
I catch a glimpse of heavenly walls,
Where rays of sunlit topaz mix
With deeper veins of sardonyx.
Thus might thy soul resplendent shine
Beside the colder glow of mine !
Lavinia, wilt thou not wait
For me, within the golden gate !

BALLAD OF THE BLITHE QUARTETTE

[LOCKER, DOBSON, GOSSE, AND LANG.]

THIS is the poet's twilight shade,
   When songs inspired no longer ring;
Forgot is Pan in glen and glade,
   And mute, Apollo's glorious string.
   The muse divine hath taken wing
To unfrequented heights — and yet,
   While critics keen are caviling,
We hear them play — the blithe quartette!

With harps from morning-lands estrayed,
   And tunes as joyous as the spring,
A minstrel lover's serenade,
   The rondel of some jovial king,
   A melody whose swirl and swing
Our pulses all a-dancing set,
   A jester's catch without its sting,
We hear them play — the blithe quartette!

Staccato measures deftly made
   Afar their brilliancy to fling —

Perfection of the art essayed,
    Each note a flawless, crystal thing;
    Gay chords with laughter echoing,
And some that leave our eyelids wet;
    Life's heartsome lays, to which we cling,
We hear them play — the blithe quartette!

ENVOY.

Kind sirs, let us this solace bring
    To ease our souls of vain regret:
Though noontide poets cease to sing,
    We hear them play — the blithe quartette!

MY LADY OF MAKE-BELIEVE.

My lady hath realms of wide domain;
  Castles and palaces proud and fair;
A dungeon-cell, with a clanking chain,
  A lonely turret, with winding stair.
Here kings and courtiers in homage stand,
  Here prisoners sigh and wait reprieve;
And she rules with a regal sway the land,
  This marvelous land of Make-Believe.

My lady hath rank of all degrees,
  From proud Queen Bess to the Beggar-Maid;
To-day, a princess from over the seas,
  To-morrow, a gypsy tattered and frayed.
She hath countless titles that come at call,
  Or unto her courtly station cleave;
And one that suiteth her best of all; —
  My winsome Lady of Make-Believe!

My lady hath garments of stiff brocade,
  Roses of silver bespangle them o'er;

Her fan for the Queen of the East was made,
   Her train — it traineth a yard or more.
She hath silks and ribbons in rich array;
   The looms of Lyons her velvets weave;
And she weareth them every single day —
   This vain little Lady of Make-Believe!

She hath Medici collars and Honiton lace;
   She doeth her hair à la Pompadour;
Or hideth her "bangs" and her gleesome
      face
   Under the bonnets her grandame wore.
She hath bracelets, and charms, and chains, and
      rings;
   For jewels like hers a king might grieve;
To pauper and prince her wealth she flings —
   My gracious Lady of Make-Believe!

She hath waiting-women who stand and wait,
   Or hasten to do her bidding sweet;
She hath slaves who kneel at the palace gate,
   And fear the stamp of her tiny feet;
And many a knight who for one sweet glance,
   Would wear her favor upon his sleeve,
And shiver for her the stoutest lance —
   My haughty Lady of Make-Believe.

"Illusions are vain," doth the preacher say?
  "Empty and idle is all that seems"?
"The pageant passeth"?   Ah, well! for a day
  No shadow hath dimmed her blithesome
      dreams;
And gentle and pure are her guileless arts,
  Though her name should ever the world de-
      ceive;
For truest of true, in her heart of hearts,
  Is my winsome Lady of Make-Believe.

WILD VIOLETS.

When clouds from April skies have rolled,
Though earth be chill and winds be cold,
And woodland ways still lone and wet,
I seek the first wild violet
That blooms above the fragrant mould.

Thy mien is proud, thy pulse controlled;
Thou wear'st the regal roses sold
In city marts; and yet — and yet —
Thou wert thyself a violet
In those enchanted days of old.

So send I — am I over bold? —
This gift to grace thy bosom's fold;
Believing if thy hand doth set,
Against thy heart, a violet,
An old-time love may yet be told.

58

JUNE.

The month of roses, forever fair,
   Radiant, miracle-working June!
Laden with color and perfume rare,
   Set with the song of birds atune!

The blue of the West is in her eyes,
   The kiss of the East on her dewy mouth,
While damask and white on her bosom lies
    The bloom that breathes of the burning
      South.

With joy of living, her voice beguiles;
   Love, at her touch, all nature sways;
Her gladsome, glorious beauty smiles,
   And lo! the coming of perfect days!

JULY.

She comes elate her own to seek,
   The peerless queen of summer days,
The warm winds kiss her ruddy cheek,
   The earth with fruitage lies ablaze.

Through paths of endless bloom she walks ;
   With tilted lance the grasses stir ;
The cornflowers bend on slender stalks
   In sweet obeisance unto her ;

While troops of daisies, born afield,
   Their dainty petaled rims unfold ;
And like a royal legion yield
   For her their glowing hearts of gold.

AUGUST.

WHITE noons are languorous with the light;
   Parched lands lie sterile in the dearth,
Day unto day and night to night
   Pulsating with the throes of earth.

Only in some remote retreat,
   Hidden afar from haunts of men,
Faint signs of life our senses greet, —
   A whir of wings from cooling fen;

Or, where the sheltering shadows fall,
   The water-lily bares its breast;
And slumberous perfumes rise and call
   A world resistless back to rest.

A ROSE IN AUTUMN.

O BOUNTEOUS Summer, we take thy bloom,
　Thy wealth of roses, and fling them by, —
Petals of flame with their depths agloom,
　And, " Largess, largess ! " ever cry.

But some late morn when the gray mists rim
　The meadows beyond the garden close,
We kiss the ghost of the frost-flower dim,
　And pledge our hearts for one perfect rose.

62

TRANSMIGRATION.

OUTSTRETCHED and stark within his icy shroud,
    The Old Year said:
"The hour has come! Thrust back the surging
    crowd,
       I too am dead!

"Ended alike the joy, the sin, the woe;
    All struggles cease;
Into the Past let me unhindered go,
    And rest in peace."

The Old Year's soul with Time stood face to
    face,
    Encircled fast;
"The Past," saith Time, "hath no abiding
    place!
      There is no Past!

"There is no New Year! This, a myth to fill
    The minds of men!

63

Thy doom is transmigration! Thou must still
    Be born again,

"Again and yet again, in some new guise,
    Till changed within,
The Old Year from its sepulchre shall rise
    Unstained by sin.

"Then in its primal purity at rest
    All time shall be
In that Nirvana of the ages blest,
    Eternity."

The solemn bells of midnight cease to toll;
    White-robed and pale,
The Old Year riseth as a new-born soul;
    And men cry: "Hail!"

A MOUNTAIN HERITAGE.

I own and possess it,
  This mountain of mine !
Exultant, I bless it,
  In shadow and shine !
For the Titans that bore it,
  And flung it on high ;
For the stars that gleam o'er it,
  Serene in the sky !
For its shadowy, solemn,
  Gray forests of pine ;
For each moss-rifted column,
  In storm-shattered line ;
For the sweep of its valleys,
  Its dim, haunted glen,
Where the elfin-king rallies
  His green-hooded men ;
For the ripple and laughter
  Of brooklet and breeze ;
For the thrill that comes after,
  Aloft through the trees ;

For the rocks split asunder
  By frost and by sun,
For the streams that glide under,
  Green, amber, and dun,
And crown with their fountains,
  Life-giving, divine,
This mountain of mountains,
  Majestic — and mine !

My fathers bequeathed it
  From sire unto son ;
They living received it,
  And passed one by one
To glad heights eternal ;
  But hoary with age,
In sunlight supernal,
  Their last heritage,
The mountain remaineth
  In grandeur alone ;
Its glory ne'er waneth,
  Its wealth is its own.

The gay world, emboldened,
  Prays, " Yield of your heights,
Your sunsets engoldened,
  Your summer-land lights !

Let us make us proud portals
  Of cedar and pine ! " —
Stay ! These be Immortals !
  These giants of mine !
And the great builder crieth :
  " Give, give of your trees,
For the stout ship that flieth
  The sail on the seas !
Let us bend their heads hoary
  For keel and for mast ! " —
These kings in their glory ?
  These priests of the past ?
Ah ! the gods in their passion
  May strike at their heart,
But man shall not fashion
  Their shape to his art !

I own and possess it,
  This heritage blest !
With the winds that caress it,
  The light on its crest ;
With the far blue above it,
  In infinite line ;
I own and I love it,
  This mountain of mine !
But comes a heart weary
  Of worldly bequest,

All wistful and teary,
  And longing for rest,
For the balm and the healing,
  In fragrance that fall,
For the welcome revealing
  The great Soul of All;
For nature's still places,
  For solitude's bar,
For God's boundless spaces,
  Above and afar;
For the sunset's last ember
  O'er forests of pine, —
Dear heart, then remember,
  The mountain is thine!

GOLDENROD.

O GOLDENROD — wild, lavish goldenrod!
Thou glad perfection of the summer days!
    Lift up your tasseled heads
And nod to me, as in the old-time ways!
Shake out the gold-dust from your tufted
      threads,
    And dip and nod!

Yes, I remember how the warm skies hung
Above the meadows that were all astir, —
    Luxuriant with your bloom!
How waxen-sweet the crested blossoms were,
Like flaming censers, fed with rare perfume,
    And softly swung!

And there beyond the stretch of rugged sod,
Which bares its tawny breast unto the sea,
    The thick brown alders grow,
And hide the wall on which was placed for me,
All wet with dew, so many years ago,
    Bright goldenrod!

Love's first shy gift, from sun-browned, boyish
    hands !
True hands and brave, in toilsome, work-day
    fields
    Grown strong ; yet still to me
Bearing the bloom the choicest season yields,
As on we fare where noontide shadows be
    In pleasant lands.

But I have longed through all the happy years,
O glad, wild flower, upon these slopes aglow,
    Once more to see you swing ;
I did not think your breath would choke me so !
I never dreamed your dainty airs could bring
    These sudden tears !

SONG OF THE JENNIE.

Where skies are fair the Jennie rides
   The bosom of the sparkling lake ;
The breeze sweeps down the mountain-sides,
Kisses the water as it glides,
   And ripples in her wake.

We hear the stroke of rhythmic oars,
   By dainty hands dipped low and swung,
As skims the boat by sunny shores,
And where the gurgling stream outpours
   Its rocks and reeds among.

Or where thy mirrored crest beguiles,
   O granite-browed Megunticook,
She breaks the green pool into smiles,
And nestles midst the faery isles
   That to thy fastness look.

And when, at dusk, one white star shines,
   Above the blue lake's mystic rim,

The Jennie sweeps across the lines
That fringe the shadowy shore of pines,
  Into the twilight dim.

And glad ears catch the liquid notes
  Borne lightly on the joyous air ;
O bonniest of bonny boats,
With thee she sings, with thee she floats,
  The maid with shining hair !

Keep loving watch, O glorious star,
  Above the mountain's purple crown,
Till swings the boat within the bar,
And kindly from thine heights afar,
  O great Megunticook, look down !

ENSHRINED.

ADOWN the avenue of stately trees,
      I sit and gaze and gaze !
There is no love-song in the autumn breeze,
      No dream-light in the haze.
The golden glory of the dying leaves
      Lies trodden in the dust ;
The scarlet creeper droppeth from the eaves
      At every fitful gust;
The dark, wild ivy in its doom receives
      The mildew and the rust.

Oh, glad, exultant Spring ! and only this
      For many a promise given !
Oh, blighting sense of utter dreariness
      After the breath of heaven !
The cloud-like phantom of a waning moon
      Follows the setting sun ;
The distant owlet croaks his dismal tune
      In caverns dank and dun.
Oh, ghost of idle days — to come so soon,
      As though the race were won !

73

I have no new-made grave on which to fling
      My soul, in vain regrets,
Or wait until the luring airs of spring
      Bring back the violets ;
I only ask for this lost year of mine
      A sacred, fresh, new tomb ;
I have no fear that ever touch of time
      Its treasure will consume ;
I bring sweet spices here, and oil and wine,
      And many a rich perfume.

Beneath the pyramids the kings lie down,
      And in their fastness sleep ;
Beneath the floods the royal lilies drown,
      And none are left to weep.
Embalmed in state, alone and silently,
      Shall lie my crownèd dead,
My regal year, whose grandeur none shall see,
      For whom no tear is shed ;—
How long his promised length of days shall be,
      The Lord hath never said.

SPOKEN AT SEA.

ALL men go down to the sea in ships :
With a trembling hand and faltering lips,
We spread our sails on the deep unknown,
Each for himself and each alone.
   The strong tide floweth unceasingly ;
   God only knoweth our destiny.

And ships may meet, as yours and mine ;
With a tender gleam, the deck-lights shine ;
There are wind-swept words of kindly cheer,
A song, a smile, perchance a tear ;
   Then on, for the ever-hurrying sea
   Sings of the shadowy yet-to-be !

And the light dies out of each shining track ;
The course was chosen ; we turn not back ;
No hands are clasped o'er the soundless blue,
But hearts though severed may yet be true ;
   And a sweeter story ne'er shall be
   Than of memory's ship-lights spoken at sea.

THE BATTLE-SONG.

A Ballad of Brittany.

1758.

With eyes afire and hearts aflame, the valiant
    peasant host,
From Tréguier and good Saint Pol, marched
    up the Breton coast.
"Sing us our father's battle-song," the stand-
    ard-bearer said,
"And let the cursed invader know, 'King Ar-
    thur is not dead!'
The song that every mother's tongue and every
    maiden fair,
A thousand years and more have sung from
    Orne to Finistèrre!
The song by which the Cymric chiefs their
    ancient battles won,
That we, as they, the foe may slay before the
    turn of sun!
'A foeman's heart for every eye! a head for
    every arm!'

The valleys and the mountain-tops know well
    the wild alarm !
'Three lives for one!' by grassy mound and
    by the cromlech's mould,
And 'blood for tears,' shall dew the ground as
    in the days of old !
Sing, comrades mine ! the sea-lights shine
    where flies the banner red !
As long ago, we greet the foe : ' King Arthur
    is not dead ! ' "

With eyes afire and hearts aflame, from o'er
    the English Sea,
A band of brave Welsh mountaineers marched
    down through Brittany.
" We strike for England," was the cry, " before
    the turn of noon,
But live or die, fling out on high the ancient
    battle-tune !
The song that for a thousand years has floated
    on the gale,
From Snowdon heights and Harlech lights to
    far Glamoran's Vale ;
The song our Celtic sires loved, in days that
    long have fled,
That mothers to their first born sung : ' King
    Arthur is not dead ! ' "

And like a royal chant of old, rang out the
  martial strain ;
But hark ! — a pause — and from afar comes
  back the grand refrain !
And where the borders of Saint Cast their
  broken ridges trace,
The invader and the Breton-born stood grimly
  face to face.
" King Arthur is not dead ! " the one in rhyth-
  mic cadence cries ;
" King Arthur is not dead — not dead ! " the
  Breton host replies.

" Halt ! fire ! " the English captain shouts.
  Nor hand nor musket stirred ;
And " Fire ! " rings down the Breton lines ;
  yet no man heeds the word ;
For all who march to Arthur's call are of one
  kith and kin ;
No feud have they, no foe to slay, no strife to
  lose or win !
But heart to heart, and hand to hand, the
  weeping soldiers stood,
Whose one ancestral song had proved their
  common brotherhood.
Ay ! tears for blood ! Thus shall it be from
  Orne to Finistèrre,

With love for hate, from Snowdon's hills unto
    Glamoran fair,

And peace for strife, throughout the world, and
    right in place of wrong,

When men shall learn their brotherhood
    through one Immortal Song.

PROPHET AND POET.

I.

THE PROPHET.

SCENE IN THE COURT OF THE ROYAL PALACE
AT GRANADA, A. D. 1194.

PROPHETIC silence broods o'er Andaluz:
The stately palms lift up their crownèd heads
And listen, listen ; while the vines, deep set
In golden mellowness, cling close and mute
Unto the warm green bosom of the hills
In hushed expectancy.   Beyond the far
Sierras, moon and stars swing low and fade,
Not in a liquid opal-tinted dawn
Whose blue and crimson meet and blend and
      pale
And faintly glow again, but in the full,
Triumphant coming of a day that bursts
Upon a waiting world in perfectness,
And spreadeth sunshine royally ! Ay, such
A day as only breaks when Moslem kings
Are born !

      All through the night each gilded dome

And frosted minaret had flashed, alight
With heaven's transcendent glow; for signs
   more rare
And potent ne'er had hung o'er princely head
Than marked the advent of the babe vouch-
   safed
To Nasar's line — the babe Alhamar named!
And when, at dawn, the jagged mountains
   veiled
Their sharp, stark faces in the roseate hues
Which make the hoary hills forever young,
When shrill-voiced sentinels aroused the world
From slumber unto prayer, then all the grand,
High places, which for aye shall tell that God
Is great, made answer to a new refrain
In solemn ecstasy.   From crag to crag,
Each rock set Atalaya flung the shout,
And ere the Darro's silver threaded net
Had caught the noontide glimmer in its mesh,
Granada's farthest vale had learned —"There is
No God but God!" and — "Nasar's king is
   born!"

  Throw open wide the royal gate!
The court astrologers unto the spacious hall
   descend;

While eager multitudes their coming wait
And like tall, wind-swept rushes sway and
bend
 In feverish delight.
 The priestly hems,
Broidered with Oriental signs, and thickly,
quaintly hung
With fringèd gold and many brilliant gems,
Clink down the marble stairs and trail
among
 Close-crowded tunics, cool and white.
 "Who greater is," the prophets cry,
"Than Prince Alhamar, or shall be, while
stars portentous roll ? "
And slow they swing their mystic wands on
high,
And dip their sharpened cusps to mark the
scroll
 With his nativity.
 "A proud career
The stars predict for Nasar's prince," they
say. "The years shall send
Him every kingly gift; and bard and seer
Recount his fame till Moslem kingdoms end ;
 A prince beloved in peace is he :
 Invincible in war ! "

"El Ghalib!" all the people shout. "El Gha-
      lib! Conqueror!"
"There is no conqueror save God!" In calm
And measured accents, as from one who stands
Serene above the tangled ways of men,
The solemn words upon the startled throng
Descend. The mad, wild clangor ends in
      strange,
Oppressive silence. Who shall dare gainsay
The truth of Moslem Writ? Yet as the gaunt,
Gray-bearded man, bowed down with age and
      leagues
Of dusty travel, stands within their midst,
The court magicians glance at him askance;
Then towards the Kebla turn their steadfast
      eyes
As if for morning prayer. So all the throng,
In mocking mood, makes way and stands
      agape,
While they who catch the scornful cue exclaim,
"Lo! here a prophet is! See how his staff,
Crooked like an Almucantar's rod, hath turned
Unto the East! Behold his girdle wrought
Of leathern fragments, set with Cufic signs
Long since forgot in Araby; and robes
So ancient in their grimy woof, the great

Mohammed may himself have worn them ere
He slept!   A son of wonders truly he!
Shall he not prophesy?"

                                Ay! prophesy!
Who fitter for the task than he who seven
Times seventy rounds hath made with san-
        daled feet,
About the Caaba's shrine, and prostrate, kissed
The Holy Stone with each required prayer?
Who, living threescore years and ten, hath
        drank
From Zem Zem's waters once for every year,
And home returning, hung his open tent
With Mecca's aloe-bloom?   To what more true,
More faithful son should Allah grant the gift
Divine of prophecy?

                        Closer around
The aged seer crowded the mocking throng.
The wrinkled face shone fair.   The feeble
        frame
Majestic grew through inspiration's light.
"O Moslems!   Ye do well to learn of great
Alhamar's reign!   Stretch out your eager arms
And clasp the vision of exultant power
That cometh at his beck!   Let flash your keen
Blue scimitars, and shout as pleaseth men

For triumphs yet to be ! But days are near
When Islam's haughty sons shall learn that
     pride
Has heights before unknown ; and victory
Is only his who conquers in defeat.
Beneath a crown all kings are great ; but he
Who crownless makes the nation's foe its friend
Alone hath royalty ! O children, born
Of princes and by prophets taught, think ye
Of this when unto Islam's hated foe
The great Alhamar kneels !"

                Like winds
Among the rustling corn, a murmur rose
And ran. " A Moor to unbelievers yield !
A Moslem monarch sue for grace at whose
Glad birth-hour Jupiter hath smiled ? A son
Of Beni Nasar kiss the dust while gleams
The Moorish spear ? " And loud and louder
     grew
The clamor of the faithless multitude,
By sneers and threats of wily craftsmen led,
Till mad with frenzied unbelief, they hurled
The Prophet from the city's outer gate,
And stoned him unto death.

              This is the tale
Of Aben Hared. Unto God all men
Belong. To Him may we in peace return !

II.

THE POET.

TIME, TWO HUNDRED YEARS LATER: IN A COURT
OF THE ALHAMBRA, A MINSTREL SINGS.

Yusef of Nasar reigneth ; and the City of the
    Fountains
Like a white-robed queen is thronèd in her sun-
    lit majesty ;
And, like white-robed maids-in-waiting, behind
    her stand the mountains,
With their snowy clustered summits, keeping
    lookout o'er the sea.
And the massive, red Alhambra, with its alca-
    zar and towers,
Guards the happy, trustful Vega, stretching
    leagues and leagues away,
Content and trustful ever, though the war-sign
    lifts or lowers,
With its fiery eyes in night-time, and its smoky
    haze by day.

Secure within the valley, the cool wind wooes
    the spirit
Of the sunny tropic regions with a promise soft
    and sweet ;

But the aloes bend their heads, and the listen-
    ing vine-leaves hear it,
And tell it to the hillsides and the waters at
    their feet.

Then the noisy, dashing Darro down its rocky
    chasm dances,
And brings a hundred streamlets on the snowy
    mountains fed ;
While the blushing vineyards reddened with the
    summer's ardent glances,
Cry, "'T is we who fill the wine-cups ! Let the
    wind and sun be wed ! "

Oh ! the breath of burning fragrance that across
    the southern ocean,
Comes to greet the cool forget-me-nots and
    dewy asphodels !
Oh ! silvered grain-fields swung with an innate,
    rhythmic motion !
Oh ! tropic fruits that dip and nod like golden
    marriage-bells !

Happy art thou, fair Granada, where the North
    and South have striven
Each with its rarest offering to grace the wed-
    ding feast !

Happy hills and happy valleys, where the rug-
    ged West has given
Its furrowed cheek and bosom to the kisses of
    the East !

Blest for aye the favored city with its thousand
    towers gilded
And lifting each its minaret beneath the am-
    bient skies, —
The skies above Granada, in whose lucid
    heights are builded
The moon-tipped domes and spires of the
    Prophet's Paradise !

Thus in the Moorish court the Poet chanted,
When o'er the marble floor each slender
    column
Had marked its slanting shadow, and the
    gleams
Of moonlight fell, through fretted lace-work
    stealing,
And through the silvered traceries, revealing
The rare, quaint fancy of Arabian dreams.

He had come in, unheeded and undaunted,
Himself so like a shadow dark and solemn,

In robes of camel's hair through deserts
      trailed ;
Silent he stood with aspect stern and dreary,
Till of the revel all the throng grown weary,
Had with delight the strange musician hailed.

"Sing of Granada!" prayed the fair — the
      knighted ;
And softly dripped, in founts of alabaster,
Wine-tinted waters, while the minstrel sung ;
"Of great Alhamar!" cried the king applauding,
A song of war, his noblest triumph lauding,
In days when Cross with Crescent clashed and
      swung.

As with a flash, the poet's dark eyes lighted ;
And from its place beside the dim pilaster
He proudly caught his sweet-stringed instru-
      ment ;
No Moslem scimitar unused to sheathing,
No battle-axe of Moorish onslaught breathing,
Could to its chords a wilder strain have lent.

And turbaned knights let fall their half-drained
      glasses,
And ladies fair behind their gem-lit veiling,

The closer shrank, eager and yet afraid,
As through the dim hall, drifting like a vision,
The swift word-painting moved to airs ely-
     sian
Like pictured hangings by enchantment swayed.

They see, as men in dreams, the mountain
     passes,
And lance and banderole where wild vines
     trailing
Alone had choked the long unused defiles ;
While fair Granada, like a golden-hearted,
O'er-ripe pomegranate from its stem half-
     parted,
Within the greedy gaze of Castile smiles.

And Christian foe beneath the ramparts sit-
     teth, —
Jaen, the valiant, through the long months
     making
Its brave defense with many a fight and feint ;
But ghastly famine stalks above the moating,
And o'er the walls, thin, bloodless spectres
     floating,
Bear fateful signs to Ferdinand the Saint.

Then over all a sudden grayness flitteth
From which one form its shapeless figure
    taking,   .
Drifts like a phantom o'er the shrouded plain.
'T is proud Alhamar!   See! they catch the
    glimmer,
Beyond Jaen where festive tent-lights shim-
    mer! —
Still through the dim court floats the wild
    refrain:

Woe to Granada!   What now are the towers,
That rise from her ramparts massive and red!
Woe to Granada!   What now are her bowers
But sepulchred gardens with bloom for the
    dead!

O valleys! look upward where city lights
    glisten!
Is there no help where the white crescents glow?
O ill-fated city! look downward and listen!
Hear ye no tidings of good from below?

Ay! down from Granada a lone horseman
    goeth!
Can one avail aught where the chosen host
    fails?

Who gains from the deep sea its secret ? —
    .   Who knoweth
The soul of a king till misfortune assails?

On, on, through the night, he is breathlessly
    speeding,
On where the swift Xenil silently steals,
Still on, through the camp revel, mute and
    unheeding,
Till low at the feet of the Christian he kneels.

" I am Alhamar !   Alas, what remaineth
Of greatness, since spent is the struggle, and
    vain !
What for the proud heart or false hand that
    staineth
Granada's white marbles with blood of the
    slain !

"Thou art the Castilian !   Oh ! take as a
    token
Of Moslem allegiance the homage we bring,
But spare thou the gates of the city unbroken,
I plead for my children as King unto King !"

And back from the valley in lingering sweetness
The glad voices ring from the hills to the sea,

With the echoing song in its joyful complete-
      ness,
" Granada is ransomed ! Granada is free !"

" Thou singest well ! O dusky Arab stranger !"
The monarch said, while eyes tear-dimmed with
      pity,
Beneath long lashes tremulously gleamed ;
" Poor, poor indeed, were Islam's boasted
      cluster
Of stout-walled cities had it missed the lustre
Of fair Granada by her king redeemed !

" How wrote Mohammed in the days of
      danger ?
' To him who conquers pride, and, for the city,
Humbleth himself, doth victory belong !'
Bring forth the cups with prisoned sunlight
      shining,
Drink to Alhamar while fair hands are twining
The myrtle-crown for singer and for song !"

Then once again the flash, as glowing embers,
Long-pent and smothered, lit anew the fire
Which in the singer's dusky eyes had burned.
" Take ye your crown with scorn too deep for
      curses !

Think ye, O haughty Moors, that tinkling verses
Are fitly crowned where prophecies were
      spurned !

" Perchance the fickle Moslem still remembers
The story, handed down from sire to sire,
Of Aben Hared — blest for aye his name !
The cold, dead past forgetteth not its sorrow,
Though what ye curse to-day, ye praise to-
      morrow,
For truth is truth, forevermore the same !

" Can great Alhamar's reign be any greater,
In these fair days when Nasar's line is reaping
The glory gathered from his deeds of old ?
Can proud fulfillment, looking backward, render
Aught more ennobling, more divinely tender,
Than Aben Hared for your King foretold ?

" The scales of justice balance soon or later !
God's dew and sunshine even yet are keeping
The grasses green above the Prophet's bones ;
While kingly grace the myrtle-crown has
      meeted
For gift of song where prophecy was greeted
In years gone by, with cursing and with
      stones !

" *I from the sons of Hared am descended* —
As ye from Nasar! " — Then with one stern
 gesture   .
The singer turned, like some avenging fate ;
And 'neath the wan moon faintly drifting o'er
 them,
Nasar's proud children seemed to see before
 them
The stark, dead prophet at their city's gate.

So like a ghost whose messages are ended,
The Poet vanished, and his sombre vesture
Fluttered and faded where the darkness
 moaned, —
The awful darkness which seemed thrilled and
 beating
With scornful echoes, o'er and o'er repeat-
 ing : —
"The son of Hared — whom your fathers
 stoned ! "

GLENDARE.

THE wild torrents plunge o'er the falls of Glendare,
  The cliffs of Glendarock hang high with a
  frown,
And night from the hill-tops sodden and bare,
  In its gray sleety cloak with the storm-wind
  comes down.

Roy of the Highlands, he hastes from the seas,
  But my Lady Glendare no longer can wait ;
Like a wan, spectral shape in the shadow she
  flees,
  While the warden sleeps sound at the stout
  castle-gate.

Faster, oh, faster ! my Lady Glendare !
  Thy black-hearted lover will close on thee
  soon !
He rideth behind on the wings of the air,
  As the black-hearted tempest rides after the
  moon.

And faster, my lad, from the free Highland
   hill !
    Let each sail to the winds ! let each breath be
      a prayer !
For her life-blood runs slow and her life-blood
   runs chill ;
    She hath beckoned to death — my Lady Glen-
      dare !

She heareth the clangor of armor behind,
    The tramping of horsemen afar o'er the
      land,
But never the flapping of sails in the wind,
    Or the noise of the keel as it grates on the
      sand.

The wild torrents plunge o'er the falls of Glendare ;
    There are horsemen above, there are boat-
      men below,
But the waters have tangled my lady's bright
   hair,
    Her bosom is cold as the winter's white
      snow.

She hears not the voice of her brave Highland
    lad,
  She heeds not, she hears not, his wail of de-
    spair ;
Wrap her deftly, though late, in the bright
    Scottish plaid —
  My sweet, winsome lady, my Lady Glendare !

THE PHANTOM FLAG.

A SPOT far up the mountain,
  A strange and awesome place,
With the great deep sky o'erhanging
  The narrow, jagged space,
Whence the long, far-reaching valley
  Doth wind its way adown
Till the blue skies kiss the greensward,
  And the plains with sunlight crown.

A glorious place, where liberty
  Shall give her children breath,
Ere she sends them down below to play
  The game of life and death.
And the blue-clad, dusty army
  In its winding path stood still,
While its glowing pulses trembled
  With a wild unearthly thrill.

" Let me shout once more for freedom ! "
  The color-bearer said :

" I can hear the death-shot rattle,
 I can feel the victor's tread !
Look ! the battle-spirits gather !
 Their hot wings hover near !
When my soul goes up to glory, boys,
 I 'll plant the Old Flag here ! "

Did ye read, O Union children,
 How burst the battle clouds ?
Did ye know how fell the hero,
 'Neath the holiest of shrouds ?
Saw ye far up the mountain
 The spectral Stripes and Stars,
When the phantom arm unfurled the flag,
 And spread its crimson bars ?

To-day the Northbound traveler,
 From lips that hold it true,
Still hears the witching story
 Of the crimson and the blue ;
Of blood-stained folds that floated
 O'er the mountain's rocky height,
Of stars that paled with those of heaven
 And vanished into night.

And the mountain lad treads softly
  As he guides the cattle home,
Half in fear and half in longing, ˙
  Through the twilight's dusky gloam.
And the pious valley farmer,
  As the sunset pennons wave,
Bows a reverent head and whispers :
  " May the God of battles save ! "

WRECKED.

At early dawn,
When first the rays of Orient light
Bid glowing welcome to the star-pale morn
And sweet farewell to night;

When distant seas
Lie blue and dim beyond the emerald bay,
And peaceful wavelets coyly kiss the breeze,
The while in idle play;

When all the earth
Is fresh and brave, our ghostly phantoms flee,
And day renewed to stalwart hope gives birth
In strong reality.

And so the men
Lift up the anchor and unfurl the sails;
"Oh, speed them!" wives and children pray
again,
"Ye prosperous gales!"

And with a song
The fisherman goes sailing to the west;
For life is love, and love divinely long;
    And life with love is blest.

But with a moan,
The fisher's wife sits sobbing under breath;
For life is love, yet love must die alone,
    And loveless life is death.

O sea-gulls gray!
What mean your voices shrilling with despair,
As evening's calm drops o'er the little bay
    Beneath the leaden air?

O men with ships,
Who on the deep have journeyed up and down,
Have ye no answer for the questioning lips
    Within this quaint old town?

For night has come,
And grim portentous shapes flit wildly by;
And cowering hearts are smitten and grow
    dumb
      In silent agony.

Sweet sleep and deep
God gives to his beloved when life is o'er;
While storm-tossed waves and angry billows
sweep
For aye on life's rough shore.

Yet kindly souls,
Sweet Pity's guests, wail o'er the dead to-
day : —
Bow down, my heart, where grief's wild torrent
rolls,
And for the living pray !

NOT DEAD, BUT SLEEPING.

BEAUTIFUL Summer at rest lieth low;
  On the bare brown earth she pillowed her
        head,
And the mourners, moving passive and slow,
  Have chanted their requiem over the dead.
Her blue-veined lids are rimmed with frost,
  The light has gone from her azure eyes;
The rose from her lips forever is lost,
  Stark on the cold dark sod she lies.

The autumn flowers swung out to the breeze
  Their gorgeous bloom of yellow and red,
And whispered low to the trees, "O trees!
  Let not the world know Summer is dead!"
But the great trees drooped in the dreary spell,
  And down from the clouds of molten lead,
The shivering, quivering rain-drops fell,
  And night-winds echoed, "Summer is dead!"

Oh, never had Death in all that lie
  On his low, damp shrine a form more fair!

Oh, never were flowers so loth to die
    As the flowers that died in her sunny hair.
Fall softly, ye winding-sheets of snow,
    Fall softly over her lowly bed!
Never was earth so full of woe —
    Beautiful Summer is dead — is dead!

Dead? was the Maker mightier when
    The new-born stars first gemmed the skies?
Is He shorn of his grace, O children of men,
    Who said to the maiden, " Arise, arise?"
The arm of Omnipotence ever keeps
    The miracle age renewed in strength:
The maid is not dead! she sleeps — but
      sleeps,
    In fullness of bloom to rise at length.

AFTER THE VICTORY

THE conqueror's song hath a minor key,
The sound of a dirge in its symphony;
The voice grows hoarse with the victor's cry,
There are jarring notes when its echoes die;
"What matter?" comes back in stern reply.
The streams must run if the seas be fed,
Stout hearts be broken, so states are wed!
Red roses are crushed 'neath the soldier's
      tread,
And the white are scarce enough for the dead.
All rudely heaped in the same low grave,
Are the lovers and sons we gladly gave;
Above them the Stars of the Union wave!
And faint in the sky the war-cloud drips,
While Honor, unsullied, her finger-tips
Places, in peace, upon loyal lips.
May He, who sees with omniscient ken,
After the victory, save! *Amen!*

MERCEDES.

WE saw thee crowned ! Love came with royal
      hands
  To thee, Mercedes. All that earth held
      rare
In precious stuffs, and gems from far-off lands,
  They brought for thee ; and thou wert young
      and fair.

So sweet thy fate, the orange blossoms seemed
  More blest in every clime on this fair year ;
And maidens of their own betrothals dreamed
  More tenderly, thy wedding-bells to hear.

Yet all the while, fingers unseen had traced,
  Among the stars, thy throne and coronet :—
O sweet young queen, in realms celestial
      placed,
  For thee our eyes with blinding tears are
      wet !

We cannot see beyond the gates afar,
   Nor hear the heavenly symphony's refrain ;
We stand appalled where death and sorrow
      are,
   And weep in kinship with the heart of Spain.

THE MEED OF GENIUS.

IN THE CAMPO SANTO.

THESE pictures were Benozzo's.   His the art
 That made all Pisa jubilant, 't is said ;
And his reward ?   Oh ! list, expectant heart !
 This narrow space where he might rest when
  dead.

SIMON OF CYRENE.

UNKNOWN, unheralded, yet marked by fate,
From lands afar, he of Cyrene came,
Where mad processions led by men aflame
With rage and cursing, from the city's gate
Drag forth the Christ !
                        But yesterday, they wait
The Master with glad palms ; they shout his
        name,
They hang upon his lips.   To-day, with shame
And scourge, 't is "Crucify !"   Then, neither
        late
Nor soon, chosen of all the world, of loss
Or gain unconscious, though his Lord may die,
The chance Cyrenian comes to bear the cross.
Oh, glorious lot !   Oh, blest of passers-by !
Nor earth, nor heaven, through endless ages
        dim,
Can yield another what was laid on him !

III

A CHILD'S QUESTION.

"WHAT is it to be dead?"   O Life,
   Close-held within my own,
What foul breath in the air is rife?
   What voice malign, unknown,
Hath dared this whisper faint and dread,
"What is — what is it to be dead?"

Who told you that the song-bird died?
   They had no right to say
This to my child — I know we cried
   When Robin "went away;"
But this strange thing we never said,
That what we loved so could be dead.

Give me your hands, my only boy!
   Health throbs in every vein;
Thou hast not dreamed of earth's alloy,
   Nor stepped where guilt has lain;
O sweet young life!   O baby breath!
What hast thou now to do with death?

I even framed for thy dear sake
   Anew the childish prayer,
Lest, " If I die before I wake,"
   Should rouse a thought or care.
Mother of Christ, was this a sin —
To watch where death might enter in ?

Too late !   The Angel of the Flame
   Relentless cries : " Go hence ! "
I think of Eden's sin and shame ;
   I gaze — on innocence !
And still the curse ?   Must I arise
And lead my own from Paradise !

I see the wide, the awful world
   Loom up beyond the gate ;
I see his pure soul tossed and whirled —
   My child !   I pray thee wait !
Ask me not what the Angel saith ;
My soul this day hath tasted death !

DOLOROSA.

Madonna, hallowed with thy weight of woe,
We stricken mothers turn our souls to thine ;
We lift our faces where thy pure eyes shine,
And wonder if it eased thy grief to know
Thy son, the Christ — the dead Christ — was
       divine !

Mother of Sorrow !   Ah, but didst thou know ?
God gave us each our children, and we call
Them ours, our own !   How then could it be-
       fall
That in thy motherhood thou loved us so
Thou gavest Him, thy Babe, to die for all !

Now thou art crowned !   And yet for mortal
       sake,
In sympathy ineffable, sublime,
Thy tears fall earthward from the heavenly
       clime.
O sainted Grief ! may thy sad heart not break,
Forever laden with the woes of time !

HALLOWELL BELLS.

THE warm winds sweep from the south to-
    night,
  The breath of the springtime fills the air ;
Of odorous firs on the wooded height,
  Of burning boughs in the gardens bare.

Up the river's bank, o'er the grassy dells,
  Now soft, now loud, with a sad refrain,
There cometh the music of distant bells, —
  " To-morrow," they say, " 't will rain, 't will
    rain ! "

O grass-grown dells, ye are newly green,
  O bells, ye are far and faintly sweet,
But I think of a strip of sod between
  Two violet banks, while the winds repeat

Over and over the strain they bring,
  The rhythmic legend of olden years ;
" When ye hear the bells of Hallowell ring,
  'T will rain ! " and my eyes are filled with
    tears.

O Hallowell bells! we need not stay
   To ask of the morrow, " Foul or bright ?"
Our faint hearts sink with the dying day ;
   The clouds grow heavy!   It rains to-night!

BE MERCIFUL TO ME.

My lady lingers at her shrine
　　On bended knee, on bended knee ;
I hear her pray, "O Christ divine,
For devious, wandering ways of mine,
　　　　　Be merciful to me !"

I see her fold, childlike and fair,
　　Her stainless hands, her stainless hands,
And ask that they be cleansed to wear
The signet-seal God's children bear,
　　　　　At his commands.

I hear her plead with eyelids wet,
　　"O Heart of all, O Heart of all !
For sin that doth our souls beset,
Wilt thou in thy great love not let
　　　　　Forgiveness fall !"

I should not dare, O Saints most sweet,
　　To lift my eyes, to lift my eyes,

At her pure shrine, nor hold it meet
To kneel where she hath led my feet
      In mute surprise.

But if there need be pardoning grace
  For such as she, for such as she,
Oh, when thou bendest low thy face,
Dear Christ, from out the holy place,
      Be merciful to me !

CHRISTMAS ROSES.

When the slow dying year in silence reposes,
  Close to his chilly heart, under the snow,
Nestle the flowers we call Christmas roses,
  Born of the midwinter's passionate throe.

Up on the mountain - side, midst the dead
      grasses,
  Low at the feet of the firs in the vale,
Kissed by the winds from the sunny south
      passes,
  Blown by the breath of the fierce northern
      gale,

Ever thou springest in magical splendor,
  O miracle-blossom, perfect and pure ;
Daring thy destiny, brave and yet tender,
  Strong to resist and as strong to allure.

And thou art a Christmas rose, O my white
      flower !
  Cold is the outer world ! Whence dost thou
      bring

Warmth that is richer than summer's rare
    dower,
    Airs that are sweeter than perfumes of
      spring?

How is the smile born of dearth and of sorrow?
    Whence has life's blessedness wrought out
      its claim?
I gaze in thy glad eyes to-day, yea, to-morrow,
    And read there thine answer forever the
      same.

Keep, then, the nosegay of fair Christmas
    posies,
    Plucked from the breast of the midwinter
      snows;
Life has no secret but nature discloses;
    Mine is the lesson, sweet; thine is the rose!

THE WORLD'S VERDICT.

AT youth's glad morn, when o'er the shining
    plain
  No shadows fell to dim life's roseate glow,
  Toying with grief, the singer feignèd woe,
And sang to men a melancholy strain.
So merry maskers, for sweet pity's sake,
  Paused in the revel and let fall a tear ;
  Aghast they stood while passed the phantom
    bier,
And cried, "Oh, list ! some lone, sad heart
    doth break ! "

When sorrows came, not softly one by one,
  As shades at twilight on a day serene,
  But tempest-tost with not a ray between
The drifts of darkness deepening into night ;
When from the singer's soul, by torture wrung,
  Escaped in accents keen one bitter wail,
  The kind world mused, and said : " A plain-
    tive tale !
And yet, good masters, is it not o'ersung ? "

THE OLD HOMESTEAD.

Substantial and square and roomy,
　　It stands on the hillside green,
And the giant elm-trees guard it,
　　While sifting down between

The woof of their netted branches,
　　The sunbeams flit and fall,
Or the drift of the tangled shadows
　　Tenderly drapes the wall.

'T is the old familiar homestead ;
　　Its doors stand open wide ;
One looks to the light of morning
　　And one to the sunset side ;

But cometh the guest from the eastward,
　　Or cometh he from the west,
The broad hall gives its welcome,
　　Its welcome and its rest.

The farmer sits at the threshold,
　　In the prime of his manhood still ;

He has wrestled with toil, and conquered
  By the might of his hand and will.

He looks abroad o'er the valleys
  Where the tawny cattle graze ;
On the hay-fields green for the mowing ;
  And thinks of the olden days,

When the pastures were rough with stubble,
  Lichen and stalk and stone ;
When the meadow-lands were but marshes
  With worthless weeds o'ergrown.

Now broad are the fertile acres,
  And deep is the clover-bloom ;
And the great barns wait for its coming
  To sweeten their silent gloom.

And away to the south are the orchards
  By dew and the sunshine fed,
Till the apples grow round and mellow,
  Russet and gold and red ;

Red-ripe and russet and golden,
  They fall in the grasses fair,
And the sound of their monotone music
  Throbs on the exquisite air.

And sweeping afar are the grain-fields
Wind-tossed into silvery spray,
And circled by woodland and forest,
Sombre and old and gray.

While beyond it all is the picture,
Burned deep in the sunset dyes,
The shores in the purpling distance,
Close in whose shadow lies —

The stretch of beautiful water,
A molten shimmering plain,
The lake — but one of the thousand
That mirror the hills of Maine !

What wonder the eyes of the farmer
Grow dim with the trace of tears !
Here is bread for his children's children,
And warmth on his hearth for years.

Here is richness and health and beauty,
Blessings that never shall cease;
Within and without abideth
The plenteousness of peace.

O State beloved of the Pine Tree,
We pledge thee our troth again !

'T is the struggle with thy stern nature
  That makes us women and men.

The olden paradox brightens,
  Thy barrenness is our health ;
Thy granite heart is our glory;
  Thy poverty is our wealth.

Dip low the old-time well-sweep,
  Hallowed with sun and with rain.
Let us drink, with lips that are loyal,
  One toast : To the homes of Maine!

AVE ET VALE.[1]

SHRINED in our hearts, forever fair, there stands
 A pillared temple rising to the sun ;
Not grander were the courts of Eastern lands,
 Not prouder was the peerless Parthenon.

Here open vistas led through all the earth,
 Here Knowledge sat enthroned with starry
  crown ;
Here all the glorious dreams of youth had birth ;
 Here let the heavens their solemn secrets
  down.

O happy temple on the sloping hill,
 We hear afar thy softly ringing bell,
And send, in answer, words that throb and
  thrill, —
 Ave et vale ! Greeting and farewell !

[1] Written on the remodeling of the old Hallowell
Academy, founded in 1791.

Farewell! unto the old familiar gates,
   The stately columns and the halls of yore ;
Hail ! to the newly risen fane that waits
   With all the future beckoning at the door.

Hail ! to the tread of countless eager feet
   That come and go the symphony to swell ;
Hail and farewell! unto the phantoms sweet,
   That haunt thy shades, belovèd Hallowell.

Fair, olden city, on the river's shore,
   Thou through a measured century hast kept
The grand inheritance our fathers bore,
   When to thy wilds across the seas they
     swept.

And prized with liberty of life and faith,
   Thy honored schools their proud traditions
     tell,
Long mayst thou hear the echoing strain that
     saith :
   Ave et vale ! Greeting and farewell !

MIGNON.

O WONDROUS Mignon! thou who never wert,
  Yet strangely art, and evermore shalt be,
While throbs the deep, inevitable hurt
  That links thy young soul with humanity!

We know thy witching, half-repellent grace
  That ever lures and never satisfies;
The weird, elusive beauty of thy face,
  The nameless charm within thy tender eyes.

Only the child of genius and of art,
  The rare creation of the master's brain!
Yet still in life thou hast a living part;
  A crownless queen, thou rulest thy domain.

From out the happy Southlands thou didst
    come,
  Glad as the sun — gay child of want and
    woe —
With song and music, until smitten dumb
  By love's supreme, unconquerable throe.

Then mute, unselfish, passionately grand,
  Thy woman's soul o'erleaped its worthless
    aim ;
Thy love and longing spread through every
    land ;
  Thou gav'st to hopeless, hapless love a
    name.

Mignon ! The birds, the flowers, the soft winds
    call ;
  We hear thy step while shine the stars o'er-
    head ;
Mignon ! the shadows of the Northland fall ;
  Hushed is the music, and the dancer — dead !

O love's undying, unrequited breath !
  Thou wert called " Mignon " in the Poet's
    lore ;
O longing infinite, e'en after death !
  Thou still art " Mignon " through the ever-
    more.

BECALMED.

I.

"LISTEN!" he said, "the bells are ringing,
　　Bells of the city under the sea!
Sit in the silence!　Ocean is bringing
　　A hint of its awful mystery.
Have ye not heard of the sunken city
　　Down in the underland fathoms below?
Over its towers the sea-weed is waving,
　　Dank in its streets the mosses grow.
Sprites of the water-realm fair and immortal
　　Under its sea-green arches sing —
Listen!" he said; "the bells are ringing!
　　Only the mermen see them swing."

And the good ship lay becalmed on the ocean;
　　Lazily swung each canvas fold;
All the sky was a golden glory,
　　All the sea was shimmering gold.
Ah! the dreamy, tremulous motion!
　　The long waves come and the long waves
　　　　go.

Ah ! the holy calm of the night-watch
   After the sunset's ambient glow !
The stars look down from the great deep
     heavens ;
   And the weather-bronzed sailor whispering
     tells
His strange, weird tale of the sunken city ;
   And lists for the sound of the phantom bells.

II.

That, my lad, was in days of the bygone,
   Dead in the past ere my locks were white,
Or my eyes were dim with a life-long looking
   Unto the sunset's welcome light.
Peacefully now the white-tipped billows
   Hush the sound of their angry strife ;
Patient, I wait the call of the night-watch,
   Wait, becalmed, on the sea of life.
Let me gaze o'er the storm-scarred railing
   Into the blue of the soundless deep !
Where is my white sea-lily blooming ?
   Answer, beloved, from thy silent sleep !

Is thy moss-bed soft in the sea-dells dreamy ?
   Do golden curls with the sea-weed twine ?
Canst thou gaze afar through the pale green
     twilight,

Lit by the silver star-flower's shine ?
Dost thou catch the gleam of my life's last
    sunset,
  Purple and amber, crimson and gold ?
Canst thou lift the clasp of the heavenly portal
  Over the curtain's shadowy fold ?
God's stars look down from the great deep
    heavens ;
  They sing together again for joy —
What do I hear as I sit in the silence ?
  The bells of a sunken city, boy !

WILL IT BE THUS?

How oft, escaping from some troubled dream,
   With stifled sob and eyelids strangely wet,
We hail with joy the morn's assuring gleam,
   And smile and quite forget!

Will it be thus when waking after death,
   The horror fades that we had known ere-
      while?
When all life's struggle ends in one glad breath,
   Shall we forget and smile?

NOCTURNE.

BLUE-GRAY the sea,
Ink-blue the sky,
Above one glimmering star :
And the sullen surge,
In a measured dirge,
Thunders across the bar.

A sea-gull's cry,
From far, from high,
Falls like a dying wail ;
While the beacon-track
Of the star burns black,
In the wake of a lurid sail.

What stroke ?   What bell ?
No soul can tell,
For the dread and the horror born
Of the clamorous heart of the throbbing deep ; —
But its mighty pulses rhythm keep,
And the ship rides safe at morn !

NOVEMBER SUNSHINE.

FROM the steel-gray North, the chill winds
      blow;
  Withered and sere the leaves are lying,
Torn from the birch-tree's rustling cloak,
The purpling boughs of the sombre oak,
  And the scarlet maples, dying, dying.

Prithee, O maiden, come out to me!
  Beyond the clouds so dull and leaden,
The west grows warm with a golden tinge,
Flashes and gleams through the jagged fringe,
  Where the sunset ashes redden, redden.

So breathe but a breath from thy fragrant
      lips,
  Step but a foot on the sodden grasses,
Give but a glance from thy girlish eyes,
And out of these chill, autumnal skies
  The gruesome shadow passes, passes.

Could I but keep thee so young, so fair,
    Know that thy smile would vanish never,
There were no winter, nor wind, nor woe,
Dearth of flowers, nor blight of snow,
    But life in the Summer-lands forever.

ONCE AND AGAIN.

I.

OH ! once when our love was new,
  Do you remember, my own,
How we swung on a mountain lakelet blue,
  'Mid the forest still and lone,
While the mirrored sky went drifting by,
  Through realms celestial blown ?

Swung dreamily to and fro,
  As the shimmering waters curled
Around our prow and the heavens hung low,
  And the hills shut out the world ? —
O world, thou wert far away that day,
  And our untried sails were furled.

II.

Be still, O passionate heart,
  Whilst we number the days since then !
Come, Friend of my life, once more apart
  From the clamorous ways of men !

As we count the years through our smiles and
    tears,
  Let us drift with the waves again !

For the mountain lakes stand high
  In the land where our souls have been ;
We float where the gates of heaven are nigh,
  Where the world may not come in ;
And I dream of no greater bliss than this —
  Save that which we die to win !

ATTAINMENT.

To the north, the stars; to the south, the stars;
    above heaven's vaulted ring;
And from east to west, with unerring quest, the
    constellations swing.
I see the endless, shining track, where the
    Chariot rolls afar;
Where Perseus guards, with his flaming sword,
    the gates of the Polar Star.

And ever the mighty Hercules, with an arm up-
    lifted, kneels,
As round in his glittering, sinuous course, the
    writhing Serpent reels;
And the luminous Virgin slowly glides, her
    white wings folded fast,
Till the burning heart of the Scorpion hides
    with its baleful light outcast.

The clamor of earth is hushed; no breath
    sweeps in from the misty seas;

The leaves hang mute in the lofty tower, above
    the clambering trees ;
Beneath, from the oriole's lonely nest, no glad,
    or dolorous note ;
But perfumes faint, with a vague unrest, through
    the open arches float.

I gaze in awe at the blazing dome where the
    throes of time have birth,
And the nightly Passion Play unfolds o'er the
    unresponsive earth ;
And yet I feel the sentient thrill of life through
    the vastness whirled ;
The onward, sure, resistless force, of the ever-
    circling world.

The hidden pulse of humanity is palpitant,
    strong and deep,
Though night and death, with their semblant
    charms, the senses lull in sleep ;
And I mark the space from star to star by the
    breadth of a finite span ;
I measure the grasp of the Infinite by the
    touch divine in man ;

And know that the spirit's mysteries are solved
    in each human soul ;
And the beauty of perfectness must be its crown
    at the final goal ;
So long as the marvelous heavens above bend
    over an earthly sod,
And the immanent heart of the universe is one
    with the Soul of God.